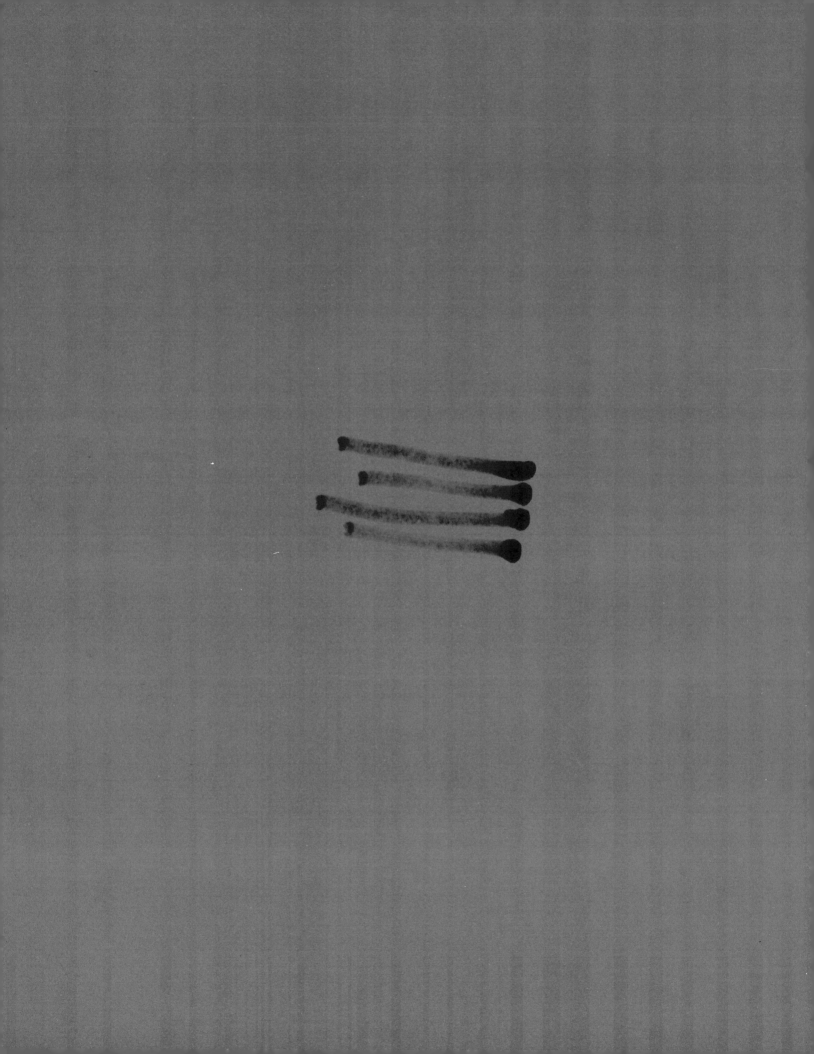

For David and Rubin, who loved it first—J. Y.

To Vera Kollontai—B. I.

SIMON & SCHUSTER BOOKS FOR YOUNG READERS
An imprint of Simon & Schuster Children's Publishing Division
1230 Avenue of the Americas, New York, New York 10020
Text copyright © 2009 by Jane Yolen
Illustrations copyright © 2009 by Bagram Ibatoulline
SIMON & SCHUSTER BOOKS FOR YOUNG READERS is a trademark of Simon & Schuster, Inc.

Book design by Laurent Linn
The text for this book is set in Aged.
The illustrations for this book are rendered in acryl gouache and watercolor.
Manufactured in China
2 4 6 8 10 9 7 5 3 1

Library of Congress Cataloging-in-Publication Data
Yolen, Jane.
The scarecrow's dance / Jane Yolen ; illustrated by Bagram
Ibatoulline.—1st ed.
p. cm.
Summary: A scarecrow happily dances away from his post one windy night,
until a child's prayer teaches him how important he is to the farm.
ISBN: 978-1-4169-3770-8 (hardcover)
[1. Stories in rhyme. 2. Scarecrows—Fiction. 3. Farm life—Fiction.
4. Prayer—Fiction.] I. Ibatoulline, Bagram, ill. II. Title.
PZ8.3.Y76Scd 2009
[E]—dc22
2008001953

The SCARECROW'S DANCE

JANE YOLEN

ILLUSTRATED BY

BAGRAM IBATOULLINE

SIMON & SCHUSTER BOOKS FOR YOUNG READERS
NEW YORK   LONDON   TORONTO   SYDNEY

An autumn eve,
The moon was high,
As yellow as
A black cat's eye.

Out in the field,
Stiff and forlorn,
The scarecrow stood
And watched the corn.

Nighttime came.
The long bell tolled
As down the rows
A wild wind rolled.

The wind blew high,
The wind blew low,
It blew the clothes
Of the old scarecrow.

His feet of straw
Began to prance,
His knees of straw
To bend and dance.

His arms of straw
Were flung about,
His mouth began
A windy shout.

He shrugged his shoulders,
And a grin
Just like a corn row,
And as thin,

Broke out along
His painted face.
He gave a leap—

And left his place.

He jogged a row
And trotted back
Along the cornfield's
Dirt-piled track,

While high above
His painted head,
The crazed and cawing
Black crows fled.

He danced past tractor
In the field,
Still waiting to
Bring in the yield,

Past cows who lay down
In the grass
And watched him
As he, silent, passed.

He danced by barn
As red as blood
And two pigs sleeping
In the mud.

He pirouetted
On the lane,
And then into
The yard he came.

Ahead he saw
A yellow light,
The family tucking
Into night.

He pressed his nose
Against the glass,
His straw feet into
Crinkled grass,

And watched a child
On bended knees
Begin a prayer
By saying, "Please . . .

". . . please bless our pigs,
And bless our barn,
And keep our chickens
Safe from harm,

Bless our cats
And bless our cows,
Bless our tractor
And our plows,

And bless tonight
Our old scarecrow
Who guards the fields
And each corn row

So that tomorrow,
When we reap,
There will be lots
Of corn to keep."

The scarecrow heard
With painted ears,
And wept a pail
Of painted tears.

Then turning, danced
Back to his field,
And right before the pole
He kneeled.

What prayers do scarecrows
Make to God?
Of sky and rain,
And wind and sod?

Or do they touch on love
Or beauty?
Do they sing of faith
And duty?

We'll never know,
Except that he,
A scarecrow
Singularity,

With one great leap—
High, high, and higher
Than any dancer
Could admire,

Slid back onto
His wooden pole,
Which—tall and straight—
Just fit his soul.

"For anyone can dance,"
Thought he,
"But only I
Can keep fields free."